# ZOMO
## The Rabbit

A TRICKSTER TALE FROM WEST AFRICA

TOLD AND ILLUSTRATED BY

# Gerald McDermott

HARCOURT BRACE & COMPANY

San Diego    New York    London

Requests for permission to make copies of any part of the work should be mailed to Permissions Department, Harcourt Brace & Company, 8th Floor, Orlando, Florida 32887.

Library of Congress Cataloging-in-Publication Data
McDermott, Gerald.
Zomo the rabbit : a trickster tale from West Africa / told and illustrated by Gerald McDermott. — 1st ed.
p.   cm.
Summary: Zomo the rabbit, an African trickster, sets out to gain wisdom.
ISBN 0-15-299967-1
[1. Folklore — Africa, West.]   I. Title.
PZ8.1.M159Zo   1992
398.2 — dc20        91-14558
[E]

The paintings in this book were done in gouache on heavyweight hot-press watercolor paper.
The display type and text type were set in Icone 55 by Thompson Type, San Diego, California.
Color separations were made by Bright Arts, Ltd., Singapore.
Printed and bound by Tien Wah Press, Singapore
Production supervision by Warren Wallerstein and David Hough
Typography designed by Lydia D'moch

BCDEF

Printed in Singapore

Zomo the Rabbit is a prominent member of the family of animal tricksters that populate the traditional tales of West Africa. These humorous stories of mischief and cunning are told to instruct as well as to entertain and have been kept alive by the powerful oral traditions of the African peoples.

There are many links between these African tales and their cultural descendants in the New World. Zomo, though separated from his origins in Hausaland, Nigeria, by an ocean and several centuries, lives on as Cunny Rabbit or Compere Lapin in the Caribbean and as Brer Rabbit in the United States.

Like tricksters in storytelling traditions around the world, the fleet-footed Zomo outwits his larger foes with guile and trickery. And like his African cousins Spider and Tortoise, he uses his wit to gain wisdom.

— G. M.

For Jimena

# **Z**omo!

Zomo the rabbit.
He is not big.
He is not strong.
But he is very clever.

Time was, Zomo wanted *more* than
cleverness — he wanted wisdom!
He went to Sky God and asked for it.

"Zomo, it is not so simple," said Sky God.
"To get wisdom, you must earn it."

"How?" asked Zomo.

"You must do three impossible things," answered Sky God. "First, bring me the scales of Big Fish in the sea. Second, bring me the milk of Wild Cow. Third, bring me the tooth of Leopard."

"I will try," said Zomo.

Zomo went to the edge of the sea.
He began to play his drum.
He played so loud his drumbeats went
down to the bottom of the sea.

Deep below, Big Fish heard the music of the drum.

Big Fish came up out of the water.
He danced on the sand.

Faster and faster, Zomo beat his drum.
Faster and faster, Big Fish danced.

Big Fish danced so fast his scales fell off.

Big Fish was naked.

Splash! He jumped back into the sea.

Quickly, Zomo scooped up the fish scales in his hat and hopped into the forest.

In the forest, Zomo climbed a palm tree.
He looked all around.
Then he saw Wild Cow.

"Ha!" laughed Zomo.
"You are not so big!
You are not strong!"

"Who is that laughing at me?" asked Wild Cow.

"It is me," called Zomo. "I say you are not even strong enough to knock down this little tree."

Wild Cow got angry.
She ran at the tree to knock it down.

Thump! She hit that tree.
But the palm tree was soft.
Her horns got stuck.

Quickly, Zomo slid down
the tree.

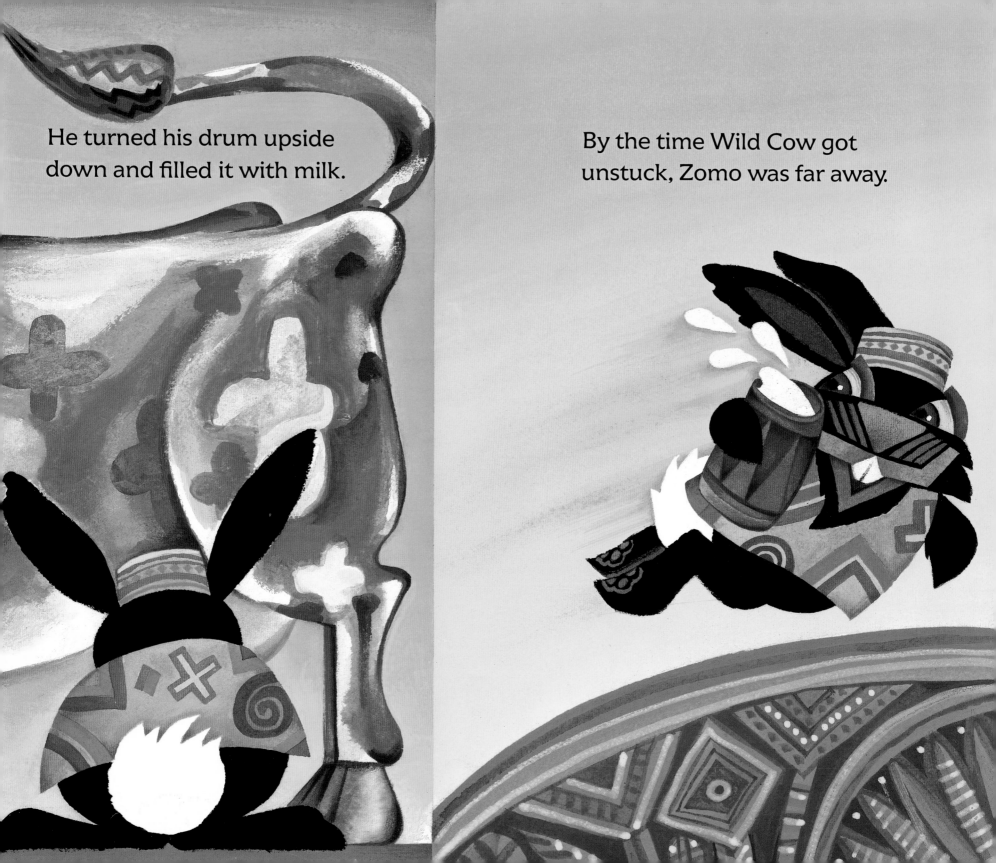

He turned his drum upside down and filled it with milk.

By the time Wild Cow got unstuck, Zomo was far away.

Zomo took the path to the top of
a high hill.
It was the hill where Leopard
walked every day.
Zomo tipped his hat and sprinkled
a few fish scales on the path.

Zomo tipped his drum and spilled
a few drops of milk on the path.

Then Zomo went to the bottom of the hill.
He hid behind a rock.

Soon Leopard came walking over the hill.
He slipped on the slippery scales and
the milk.

He rolled down the hill.

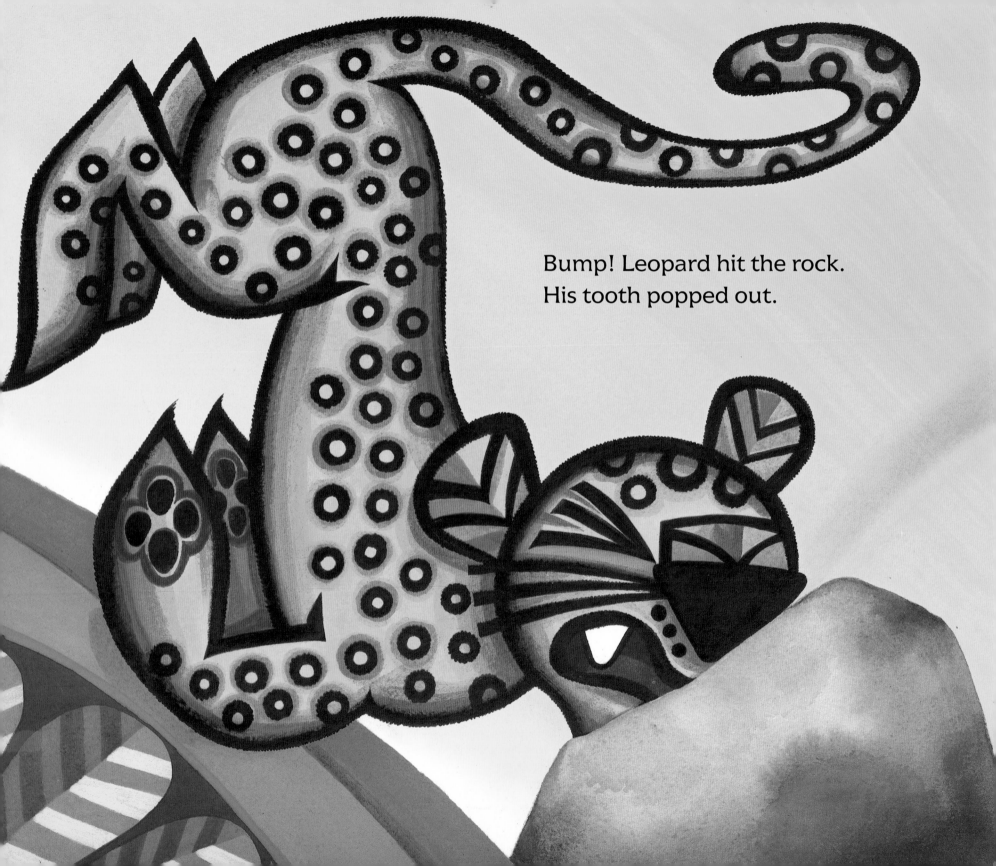

Bump! Leopard hit the rock.
His tooth popped out.

Up jumped Zomo.
He caught that tooth.
Quickly, he hopped away.

Zomo took the scales of Big Fish,
the milk of Wild Cow,
and the tooth of Leopard to Sky God.

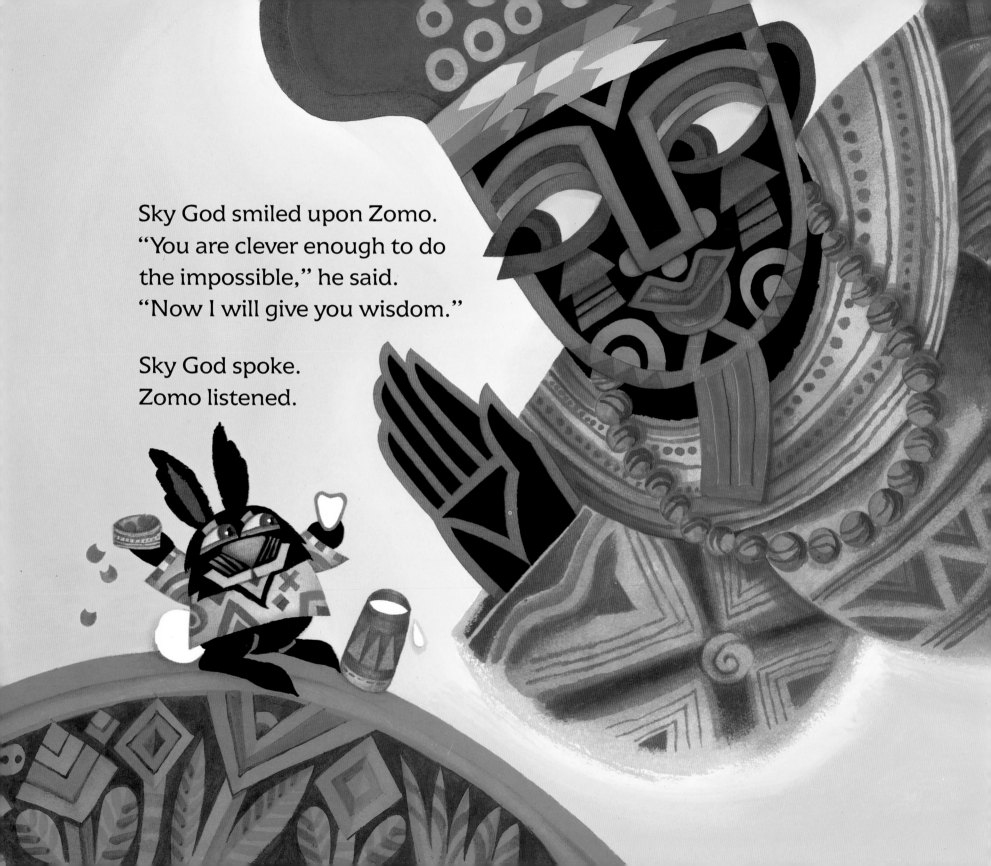

Sky God smiled upon Zomo.
"You are clever enough to do
the impossible," he said.
"Now I will give you wisdom."

Sky God spoke.
Zomo listened.

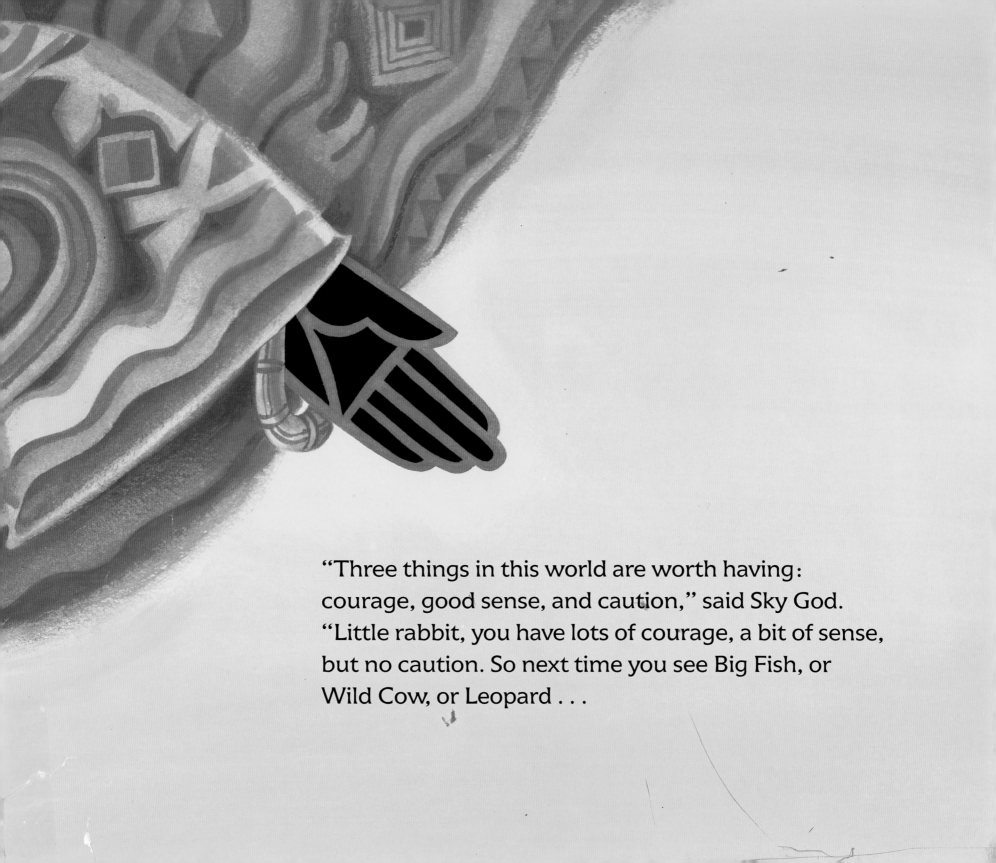

"Three things in this world are worth having:
courage, good sense, and caution," said Sky God.
"Little rabbit, you have lots of courage, a bit of sense,
but no caution. So next time you see Big Fish, or
Wild Cow, or Leopard . . .

. . . better run fast!"

Zomo is not big.
Zomo is not strong.
But now Zomo has wisdom.
And he is very, very fast.